Before reading

Look at the book cover together.
Ask, "What do you think this book is about?"

Turn to the **Key Words** page and read the words with the child. Draw their attention to the shape of the letters, noting the tall letters and those that have a tail.

During reading

Offer plenty of support and praise as the child reads the story. Listen carefully and respond to events in the text.

When a **Key Word** is used for the first time, it is also shown at the bottom of the page. If the child hesitates over a word, point to the **New Key Words** box and practise reading it together. If the word is phonically decodable, you can sound out the letters and blend the sounds to read the word ("d-o-g, dog"). Praise the child for their effort, then return to the story.

Pause every few pages and ask questions to check the child's understanding of what they have read. If they begin to lose concentration, stop reading and save the page for later.

Celebrate the child's achievement and come back to the story the next day.

After reading

After reading this book, ask, "Did you enjoy the story? What did you like about it?" Encourage the child to share their opinions.

Use the comprehension questions on page 54 to check the child's understanding and recall of the text.

Series Consultant: Professor David Waugh
With thanks to Kulwinder Maude

LADYBIRD BOOKS

UK | USA | Canada | Ireland | Australia
India | New Zealand | South Africa

Ladybird Books is part of the Penguin Random House group of companies
whose addresses can be found at global.penguinrandomhouse.com.
www.penguin.co.uk   www.puffin.co.uk   www.ladybird.co.uk

Original edition of Key Words with Peter and Jane first published by Ladybird Books Ltd 1964
Series updated 2023
This book first published 2023
001

Text copyright © Ladybird Books Ltd, 1964, 2023
Illustrations by Gustavo Mazali
Illustrations copyright © Ladybird Books Ltd, 2023

With thanks to Liz Pemberton for her contributions in advising on the illustrations
With thanks to Inclusive Minds for connecting us with their Inclusion Ambassador network,
and in particular thanks to Guntaas Kaur Chugh for her input on the illustrations

Printed in China

The authorized representative in the EEA is Penguin Random House Ireland,
Morrison Chambers, 32 Nassau Street, Dublin D02 YH68

A CIP catalogue record for this book is available from the British Library

ISBN: 978-0-241-51088-9

All correspondence to:
Ladybird Books
Penguin Random House Children's
One Embassy Gardens, 8 Viaduct Gardens, London SW11 7BW

with Peter and Jane

Holiday at the sea

Based on the original
Key Words with Peter and Jane
reading scheme and research by William Murray

Original edition written by William Murray
This edition written by Zoë Clarke
Illustrated by Gustavo Mazali

Key Words

after   all   aunt   but

from   had   holiday

house   ice cream   keep

make   must   of   our

out   read   said   sea

sun   swim   them

uncle   us   village

walk   where   which

aunt holiday house

ice cream read sea

sun swim uncle

village walk

It was the school holidays. Peter and Jane packed to go to Aunt Liz and Uncle Jack's house.

"I like Aunt Liz and Uncle Jack's dog, Kit," Peter said.

New Key Words

holiday　　aunt　　uncle　　house　　said

Aunt Liz and Uncle Jack's flat was a short walk from the sea.

"I like to swim in the sea and read on the sand," said Jane.

New Key Words

walk   from   sea   swim   read

Peter's bag, which had a bear on it, was red.

"Let's get our sun hats," Peter said.

Jane's bag, which had a horse on it, was green.

"We must pack our swim things," Jane said.

New Key Words

which   had   our   sun   must

"The sun will be out all week," Dad said.

"We can all swim in the sea!" said Jane.

"And we can have ice cream after our swim. I like ice cream," Peter said.

Jane said, "Yes! We all like ice cream."

New Key Words

    out   all   ice cream   after

"We must put all of our holiday bags in the car," Mum said to them.

Peter and Jane helped to pack the car. They had all the holiday games.

Dad packed things for all of them to read.

New Key Words

of   them

"Where are the balls?"
Jane said.

Peter looked at Tess. "I can see where they are. Tess keeps them all out here," he said.

"Come on out, Tess. You are going on holiday with us!" said Jane.

Jane picked up a ball and walked Tess out to the car.

New Key Words

where   keep   us

Peter jumped in. "Make a gap for me!" he said.

"Make a gap for us!" Mum and Dad said.

The car was full of swim things, but it was the holidays!

New Key Words

make   but

Jane looked out of the car at a village.

"This village has big houses," she said.

"But it's not Aunt Liz and Uncle Jack's village," Peter said. "They have a flat in a village near the sea. Are we near the sea yet?"

New Key Words

village

"I can see the sea and an ice-cream van!" Peter said.

Jane looked. "I can see the flat. I can see Aunt Liz and Uncle Jack. I can see them!" she said.

They all jumped out of the car.

New Key Words

"But where is Kit?" Peter said.

"Kit is in the house," Aunt Liz said. "He had a big walk in the village. After that, he had a swim in the sea."

"Can we swim in the sea?" Peter said.

New Key Words

Uncle Jack picked up the bags from the car. Jane had Tess, and Peter had the swim things.

"Which box is for swim things?" Peter said.

"This one," said Aunt Liz.

New Key Words

After they had put the bags in the house, they all walked from the house to the sea.

"Look at the sun! We must put on our sun cream and hats," Mum said.

Tess and Kit zoomed after the ball. They jumped in and out of the sea.

New Key Words

"It's Erin!" Jane said.

Peter looked. "Where?" he said.

Erin and her dad had walked to them. They had a house near Aunt Liz and Uncle Jack's flat.

"You can swim in the sea with us!" Jane said to Erin.

Jane, Peter and Erin had a swim.

New Key Words

"Aunt Liz! Uncle Jack! Look at us in the sea," the children yelled.

The sun was hot, but the sea was not!

"Let's get out," said Erin.

"Can we have ice cream?" Peter said. "I do not like cool water, but I like ice cream."

New Key Words

The children all walked up to the village.

"Can you read it, Peter?" Jane said. "Which ice cream do you want?"

"I can read it, and I want all of them, please," Peter said.

New Key Words

After they had ice cream, they walked to the boat house where Uncle Jack works. Erin walked with them.

"Where are the boats?" Jane said.

"Some of them are here," said Uncle Jack. "But I must fix them."

"Let us help you fix them," Peter said.

New Key Words

39

"Where are the paints?" Jane said. "Where are the brushes?"

"You can get them from there," Uncle Jack said.

Jane picked them up from the bench.

Peter looked at all the brushes. "Which one can I have?" he said.

"That one," said Uncle Jack.

New Key Words

41

After they helped with the boats, Erin walked home with her dad. Peter and Jane walked to the sea with Uncle Jack.

"Let's make a village from sand," Dad said.

"Yes!" Jane said. "We can make big villages and little villages."

New Key Words

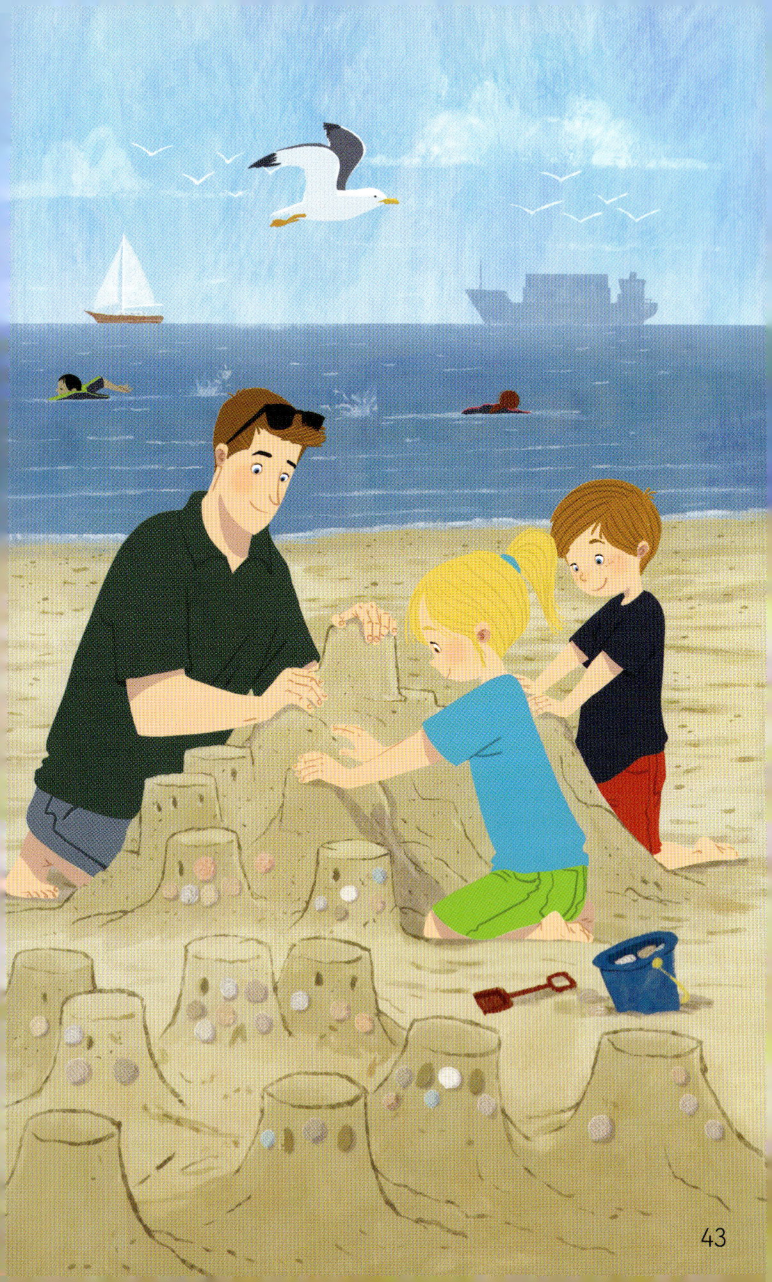

"Look at us, Mum. Look at our villages," Peter said to Mum.

But Tess and Kit jumped on all of them.

Peter was not pleased!

New Key Words

45

"Where are Aunt Liz and Uncle Jack?" said Jane.

Mum had a look. "I can see them. They walked home to make a snack for us," she said.

Aunt Liz and Uncle Jack had a box to keep things cool.

New Key Words

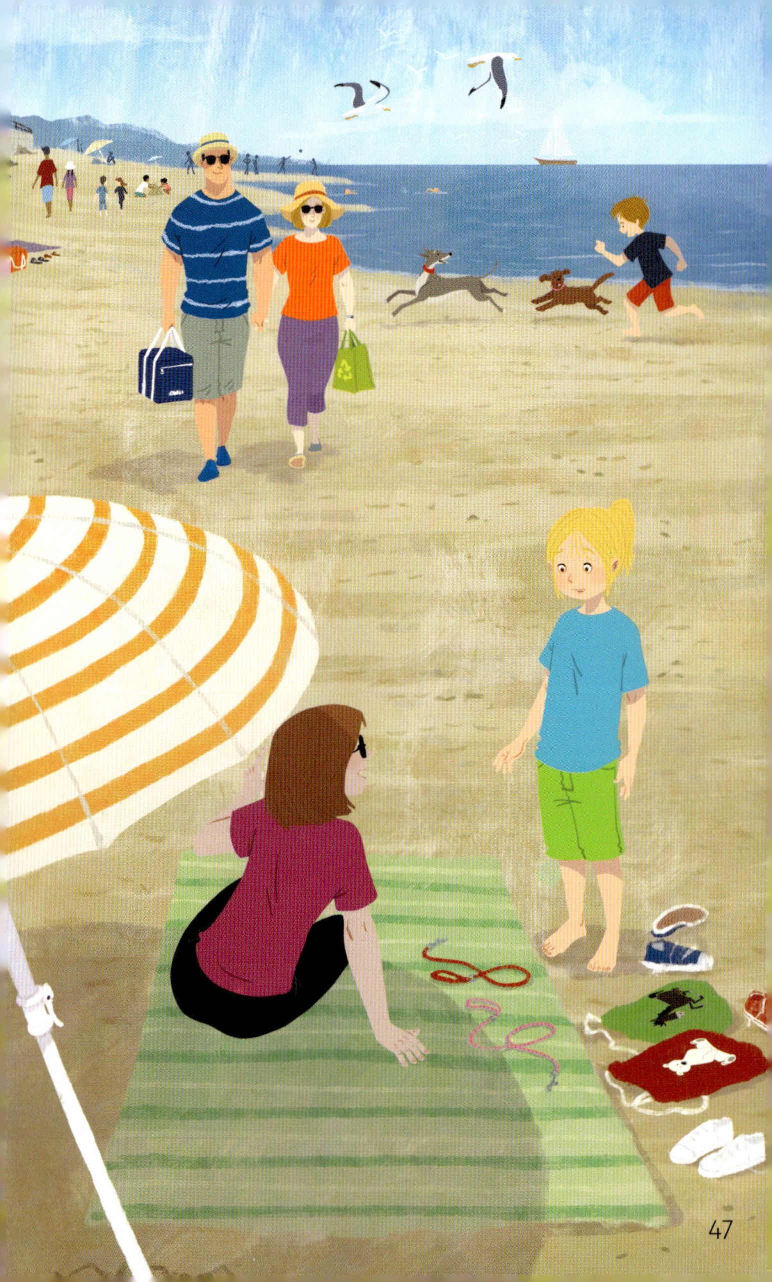

The sun was hot. They all sat down and had a rest on the sand.

"Which snack is for me?" Jane said.

Peter said, "Which snack is for me?"

The dogs had water and sat out in the sun.

New Key Words

49

After tea, Jane picked up some shells. "Can I keep them?" she said.

"Yes, you can keep some of them," Mum said.

Peter picked up all the shells. "I must keep them," he said.

"No, Peter. You must not keep all of them," Dad said.

New Key Words

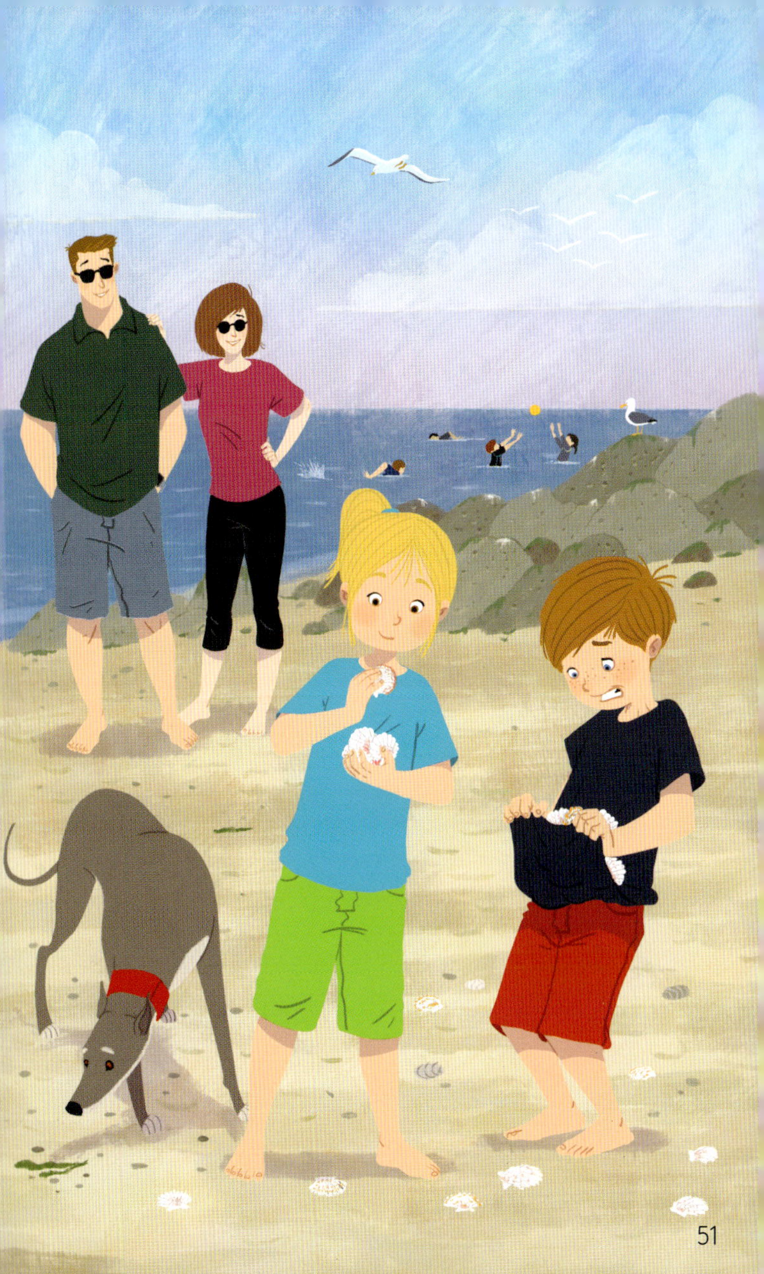

Peter and Jane had a walk.

"Our holiday in the sun is fun," said Jane. "I like the sea."

"I like holidays and the sun," Peter said. "But I like ice cream the best."

New Key Words

53

Questions

Answer these questions about the story.

1 What do Peter and Jane do at the start of the story?

2 What do Peter and Jane see from the car?

3 How do the children help Uncle Jack fix the boats?

4 What happens to the children's sand villages?

5 What do Jane and Peter pick up on the beach?